Jungle

To Mum, Dad, Keith and Alison

James
and the Jungle

written and illustrated by

Tracey Lewis

Macdonald

James's dad gave him his own patch of garden.
'What can I plant in it?' thought James.

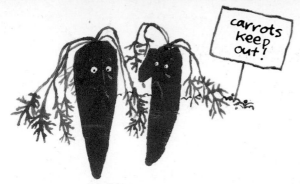

He didn't want carrots

and he didn't want cabbages.

He didn't want petunias

and he didn't want pansies.

No, James wanted a jungle, so he bought

He pulled up the weeds,

planted the seeds,

watered the ground,
and waited.

The next day when he went into the garden,
the jungle had grown up thick and green.
James went to have a closer look.

On Monday he took the shiny 50p piece that
Auntie Ivy had given him for his birthday
and went to the pet shop.

James didn't want beetles
and he didn't want bats.
He didn't want rabbits
and he didn't want rats.
He didn't want hamsters
and he didn't want cats.

'No,' James thought,
'I know what I want.'

'One terrible tiger, an enormous elephant, ten purple parrots, eight alarming alligators, a zany zebra and a snorty warthog, please,' said James.
'That'll be 50p exactly,' said the petshop lady.
'Do you want a bag?'

When they got home,
James said to the animals,
'This bit's yours.
The rest belongs to my dad.
Promise you'll stay in the jungle?'
All the animals smiled.

On Tuesday the enormous elephant knocked over the greenhouse.
'Oh no,' thought James, 'Dad will be cross.'

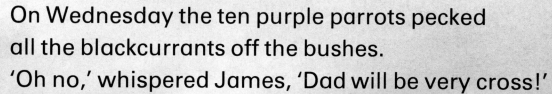

On Wednesday the ten purple parrots pecked
all the blackcurrants off the bushes.
'Oh no,' whispered James, 'Dad will be very cross!'

On Thursday the eight alarming alligators
jumped into the pond and frightened
all the goldfish.
'Oh heck!' squealed James,
'Dad will be very, very cross!'

On Friday the zany zebra ran round and round the garden,

trampling on everything, except . . .

the compost heap, which the snorty warthog
scattered all over the lawn on Saturday.

James could hardly look.

Dad's face went as purple as the squashed blackcurrants.
'I'll deal with you later!' he shouted at the animals
as he stomped off into the jungle.

'James! I know you're hiding in there! Come out!'
'Oh no!' whispered James, from behind the enormous elephant.

On Sunday the terrible tiger came out of the jungle . . .

and so did James's dad.
Nobody waited to find out
how cross he was!

Other picture books by Tracey Lewis published by Macdonald
Where Do All the Birds Go?
Oh Pebble!

A MACDONALD BOOK

© Tracey Lewis 1988

First published in Great Britain in 1988
by Macdonald & Co (Publishers) Ltd
London & Sydney
A member of Maxwell Pergamon Publishing
Corporation plc

Printed and bound in Spain
by Cronion S.A.

Main text set in Univers 55 educational face

Macdonald & Co (Publishers) Ltd
Greater London House
Hampstead Road
London NW1 7QX

British Library Cataloguing in Publication Data

Lewis, Tracey
  James and the jungle.
  I. Title
  823'.914[J]   PZ7

  ISBN 0-356-13692-2
  ISBN 0-356-13693-0 Pbk